This book
belongs to

....

Dear Logan and Keshav —
To pursuing in life
what you enjoy doing most.

For my parents.
M. B.

With very special thanks to the talented
Grahame Lyus and Artful Doodlers.

First published in the United Kingdom in 2019.

ISBN 978-1-9161469-0-7

www.saviaandspendio.com

Savia and Spendio
and the Piggy Banks

Mateja Bizjak

Once upon a time there was a sister and a brother, Savia and Spendio, who couldn't have been more different.

Savia loved to save money,

and Spendio loved to spend it.

Both Savia and Spendio
worked hard for their money.

They walked dogs around the park.

They cleaned bicycles.

They helped in the garden.

I'd like THAT cake please.

AND I WANT THAT ONE!

And so Savia's piggy bank was nearly always FULL and Spendio's was nearly always EMPTY.

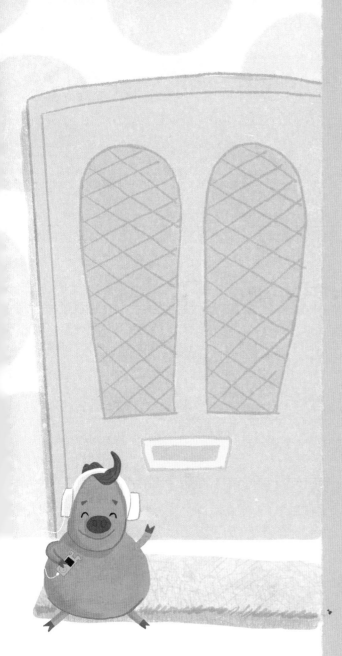

Spendio wanted to
buy an ice cream
but he couldn't.
His piggy bank
was empty.

Savia was happy with
the things she had bought,
but now her piggy bank
was empty too.

Back at home, Savia
started building.

and many nights,
just like

She worked for
many days

the inventor
from the book.

And she continued
building for

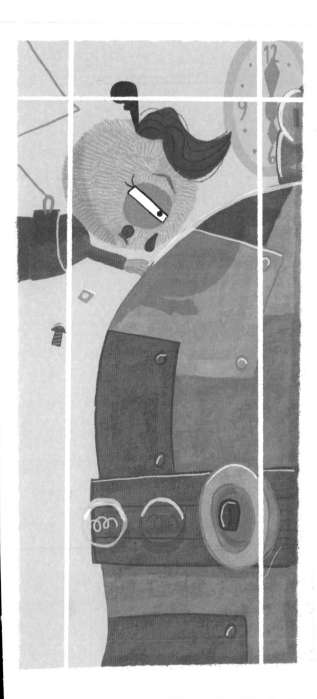

until she felt
it was just right.

many more days and
many more nights,

But where
was Spendio?

Spendio lay in bed, feeling sick
from all the sweets and cake.

"Press the button . . .! It lights up and rolls its eyes."

"Amazing!" laughed Spendio.

"It was really fun to build, but we must fill up our piggy banks again," said Savia. "Let's sell it!"

Savia and Spendio went from door to door,
asking, "Would you like to buy a funny robot?"

They asked the
dog owner.

Their
neighbour.

Their
granny.

Their teacher.

Their friend . . .

. . . and the
shop assistant.

But everyone said,
"NO, NO, NO, thank you!"

"No one will EVER buy it,"
sighed Savia sadly.

"Don't give up! We need to keep trying!"
cried Spendio.

And so they continued knocking, until finally . . .

Now Savia's piggy bank was **FULLER** than ever!

Savia bought two sweets, one for each of them, and a mountain of parts to make another robot.

Together, Savia and Spendio started building, quickly and precisely. Spendio copied every move that Savia made.

They built a robot . . .

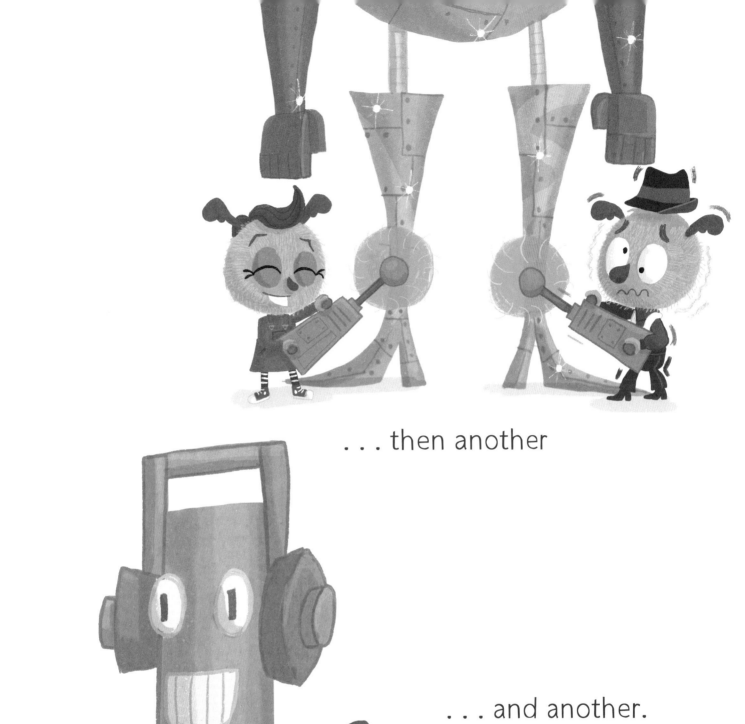

. . . then another

. . . and another.

They took their robots to a fair.
"ROLL UP, ROLL UP, to see our
wondrous robots!" shouted Spendio.

Soon there was a LONG, WINDING queue.

Everyone wanted a robot!
"We're not going to have enough!"
cried Savia as she sold the last one.

And so Savia and Spendio started building even MORE robots, and having even MORE fun making them.

And from then on their piggy banks
were NEVER empty again.

Well . . . Not quite . . .